A Beginning-to-Read Book

It's Circus Time, Dear Dragon

by Margaret Hillert
Illustrated by David Helton

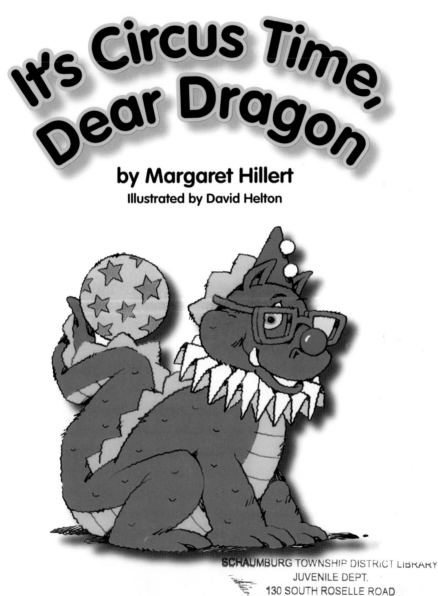

NORWOODHOUSE PRESS

DEAR CAREGIVER,

The *Beginning-to-Read* series is a carefully written collection of classic readers you may remember from your own childhood. Each book features text comprised of common sight words to provide your child ample practice reading the words that appear most frequently in written text. The many additional details in the pictures enhance the story and offer the opportunity for you to help your child expand oral language and develop comprehension.

Begin by reading the story to your child, followed by letting him or her read familiar words and soon your child will be able to read the story independently. At each step of the way, be sure to praise your reader's efforts to build his or her confidence as an independent reader. Discuss the pictures and encourage your child to make connections between the story and his or her own life. At the end of the story, you will find reading activities and a word list that will help your child practice and strengthen beginning reading skills.

Above all, the most important part of the reading experience is to have fun and enjoy it!

Shannon Cannon

Shannon Cannon,
Literacy Consultant

Norwood House Press • P.O. Box 316598 • Chicago, Illinois 60631
For more information about Norwood House Press please visit our website at
www.norwoodhousepress.com or call 866-565-2900.

LIBRARY OF CONGRESS CATALOGING-IN-PUBLICATION DATA

Hillert, Margaret.
 It's circus time, dear dragon / by Margaret Hillert; illustrated by
David Helton. — Rev. and expanded library ed.
   p. cm. — (Beginning to read series. Dear dragon)
   Summary: A boy and his dragon go to the circus where the
dragon performs some unexpected tricks on a high wire. Includes
reading activities.
   ISBN-13: 978-1-59953-040-6 (library binding : alk. paper)
   ISBN-10: 1-59953-040-6 (library binding : alk. paper)
   [1. Dragons—Fiction. 2. Circus—Fiction.] I. Helton, David, ill.
II. Title. III. Series.
PZ7.H558Is 2007
[E]—dc22   2006007093

I see it. I see it.
Oh, run, run, run.
This is something we will like.

Look at that.
Look up, up, up.
That is pretty.

5

And here come the funny ones.
Big and little funny ones.
Look here.
Look, look, look.

Now look in here.
Oh, my. Oh, my.
What is in here?

I see something big.
Big, big, big.
But I do not see you.
Where are you?

Oh, no!
What do I see now?
Come here. Come here.
You can not do that.

Come with me.
How funny you are!
But you can't do that.

Now we have to go in here.
This is where it is.
Come on in here.

This is a good spot for us.
Look what we can see.
What a good spot this is.

Oh, no!
How did you get way up there?
That is not a good spot for you.
Come down. Come down.
I did not come here to
see you do something.
I want you here with me.

Now what is this?
What do I see?
What are you on?
Get down. Get down.

You are good at that.
Yes, you are pretty good.
But I want you here.
Come here now.

Not there. Not there.
Do not do that.
I want you to come here to me.

Oh, oh.
Look at you.
Look what you have on.
You are so funny.

And now look at you.
See what you can do.
You can help this big
one jump.
My, what a jump!

But we have to go now.
Mother and Father want us.
Come on.
We have to go.

Here is something pretty.
I want a red one.
You can have one, too.

Mother! Father!
Look at us.
See what we have.

Yes, yes.
We see. We see.
What fun for you.

Here you are with me.
And here I am with you.
Oh, what a happy day, dear dragon.

READING REINFORCEMENT

The following activities support the findings of the National Reading Panel that determined the most effective components for reading instruction are: Phonemic Awareness, Phonics, Vocabulary, Fluency, and Text Comprehension.

Phonemic Awareness: The /t/ sound

Oddity Task: Say the /t/ sound for your child. Ask your child to say the word that doesn't have the /t/ sound in the following word groups:

tap, cap, pat	pod, pot, top	sip, pit, sit	pit, pat, pan
seam, seat, set	time, lime, tike	blue, to, stew	net, not, nod
riddle, little, light	kitten, card, cat	spin, spot, sport	can't, can, cannot

Phonics: The letter Tt

1. Demonstrate how to form the letters **T** and **t** for your child.

2. Have your child practice writing **T** and **t** at least three times each.

3. Ask your child to point to the words in the book that have the letter **t** in them.

4. Write down the following words and ask your child to circle the letter **t** in each word:

not	too	not	little	to	that
get	want	this	what	tail	turtle

Vocabulary: Verbs

1. Explain to your child that words that describe actions are called verbs.

2. Write the following verbs from the story on separate pieces of paper:

run	look	see	come
go	get	do	help

3. Read each word to your child and ask your child to repeat it.

4. Mix the words up. Point to a word and ask your child to read it.